D0923519

MACAROON

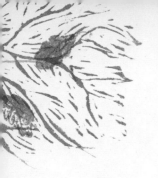

Julia Cunningham

MACAROON

ILLUSTRATED BY EVALINE NESS

PANTHEON

Text © 1962 by Julia Cunningham
Illustrations © 1962 by Evaline Ness
Published by Pantheon Books, a Division
of Random House, Inc. Manufactured in
the U.S.A.

With love from all of us

233467

THE very moment the raccoon opened his eyes he knew it was the day to decide. The pines of his forest gloomed dark against the almost brilliant oaks and maples hung with leaves of rose and pale yellow and green turning scarlet. His nose lifted to taste the air, and found it already cinnamoned with autumn, already pungent with damp earth smells like the undersides of mushrooms. Even the tips of his delicate raccoon paws were no longer quite warm.

He had a problem. If this year were like every other year in his life it would be easy enough to wander toward the village and simply wait for the first smiling child to catch him. A long winter sleep in a tree was not for him. As before, he would allow himself to be hugged and stroked and loved and taken into the child's home for the snow season, where the best place by the hearth would soon be his and his meals delivered to him in a special saucer. It was no trick at all to adopt a child. They liked him.

But all summer long the raccoon had thought of the many children he had abandoned on the first morning of spring, had heard their voices crying after him through the freedom of his freshened, newly greened woods, and he had, once or twice, been forced to hold his jaws tight between his fingers so he wouldn't answer them and become imprisoned in their world forever. He had been haunted by each round, wide-eyed face and he hadn't enjoyed the feeling. So this autumn all was to be different.

"I'm very positively not going to spend my nights holed up in a tree," he said to a very disinterested

field mouse. "Nor am I going to give up the soft
rugs and the music in the evenings and the lovely,
sneezy smell of burning logs." He glared at the
mouse. "Do you hear me?" he said sternly. "I'm
just not!"

The mouse shyly bowed himself out of sight behind a log and the raccoon was left alone with his
troubles. A crow passed overhead and squawked
something rude at the puzzled animal. The raccoon
did not reply, but the ugly sound had given him an
idea. Why not adopt a child so disagreeable, so impossible, that he would be happy to leave when the
time came? He waved his forelegs in the frosty air,
very pleased with himself, and then began to lope
slowly toward the edge of the forest. How very
clever he was! Ask a raccoon and the answer was
present before blinking. He paused to whack the
dust out of his tail between two rocks and then,
surveying the countryside, now filled with barns and
houses and standing horses, he looked out of his
bright brown eyes for an impossible child.

At first there was only the empty peace of no people at all. Then he glimpsed an oncoming procession
of small children going toward the schoolhouse in
the distant village. He recognized some of them. He
had lived in their rooms and slept in their beds. He
felt a twinge of shame at the sight of them and sup-
posed, quite rightly, that they were still wondering

what had become of their great friend the raccoon, and missing him dreadfully. None of these would do at all.

A lame fox crossed in front of him. He always spoke to foxes because they were almost as intelligent as he was.

"Good fox," he said, "have you ever met in these parts an impossible child?"

The fox halted just long enough to retort, "I'm hungry. All human creatures are impossible. You'd know that for yourself if you liked chicken dinners." And he limped swiftly away, throwing back out of the side of his bitter mouth, "Try the big house— they don't even keep chickens."

The raccoon ignored the discourtesy of the fox and, for lack of a better direction, began the three-mile journey to the mansion whose wide iron gates he could just see atop the highest hill in the valley. And, as he traveled, he began to remember a few odd fragments of gossip he had heard. There was no cat or dog within the stone walls that bordered the mansion. He smiled. Maybe because the child was difficult—and now he did truly remember, a little girl lived there, though he had never seen her in anyone else's house. And once he had found a pair of skates tumbled at the bottom of the hill, as though they had been thrown away in anger. Well, it was worth investigating, and his hopes gave speed to his legs.

He had no sooner come within peering view of the tall drawing-room windows of the four-storied, turreted house than he realized that this was his lucky hour. A sound of scolding knifed across the vast porch from inside.

"I tell you, Erika, you'll be the death of me yet! You refuse the cook's very best luncheon, and now you tell me you're not going to take a nap. I can't

punish you as you deserve because I am neither your father nor your mother."

The raccoon hopped onto the porch and pressed his right ear against the nearest pane of glass. Now he could hear the other voice, a smaller and higher one. It must be the child.

"A good thing you're not!" and the tones were even cranky enough to suit the raccoon's purposes. "I couldn't stand having them around me all the time."

He peeked in. There stood a very thin, tired-eyed woman in a gray silk dress with a white collar, and just in front of her, her face as purple as a plum, a spindling little girl.

"I wonder," said the thin woman, who the listening animal guessed must be the governess, and her voice had lost its hard edges. "Well, you do as you like about the nap. But I am going to take one and I expect you to preserve a decent silence."

He saw the governess leave the room, and the child begin to hop up and down, thumpingly, to the tune of "I Went to the Animal Fair."

The raccoon tapped on the window once, then

twice, and at last the brittle noise penetrated the bump-blast of the song and dance.

The front door clicked open and the child stepped out. At her first sight of the raccoon her face became plain white and pink again and her eyes were momentarily startled.

"Who are you?" she asked, and then remembered to be disagreeable: "And what are you doing on my porch?"

He merely snarled at her.

For answer the little girl grunted to express her extreme disgust.

He clinked his teeth rapidly together.

The child's mouth changed into a false smile. "Won't you come in?" she said, moving to one side to allow him to pass. The raccoon knew she wanted to pull his ringed tail, and he was well content. This was a fine beginning to a difficult friendship, just the kind he wanted for the winter, one he would never regret breaking off in the springtime.

He was certain to come within easy reach of her hand, and as she grabbed for his tail, he nipped at and captured the end of her thumb. He held on, being careful not to hurt her.

"You rotten raccoon!" she squealed. "Let me go!"

He obeyed, but not before he saw the purple seep back into her cheeks. Then he stalked into the house and looked about him. The depth of the rugs was quite satisfactory and the fireplace was large enough for twenty raccoons to take their repose in front of. The chairs were leather, the tables polished and smelling of cleanness, and the lamps so many that

his peculiar preference for spotlights would be well indulged.

"You act as though you planned to live here!" shouted the child indignantly.

"I do," stated the animal, speaking for the first time. "With your permission, of course," and he grinned so wickedly that he saw the shadow of a smile quirk up the corners of the child's lips. Two dimples almost formed at each side.

"You talk, too," said the child.

"I do to you," he replied, seating himself by the hearth so that she would recognize it as his place. "To no one else, so there's no use telling other people you have a talking raccoon in the house. It just causes curiosity and bother."

"It's a secret, you mean?"

He caught the glint of malice in her eyes. "No, not a secret. If it were you would enjoy telling it simply to spite me. I know." He closed his eyes comfortably.

"Don't you dare go to sleep. That's what Miss Minks is doing, and I get bored when everyone's asleep but me."

When he did not respond, she tried again.

"Don't you want to know if I have a name and what it is?"

"Later," said the raccoon, the taste of his power over this weasel of a child as sweet as a sugar lump.

"Not later—now!" and she stamped both feet. "It's Erika."

"That's a good prickly name. It suits you."

"It's not prickly at all! It's my mother's, and she's as soft as—as your fur!"

"In that case I apologize. Where is she? Anyone like my fur I would be pleased to meet."

The child hesitated. "I don't exactly know. Traveling. She takes pictures of famous people and my father writes about them. They haven't much time to stay at home."

The raccoon opened his eyes. He didn't wish to let pity or understanding spoil his pleasantly unhappy relationship with this girl. If he did, it would all end as the others had, with regret and sorrow at parting.

"Let's not talk about them," he suggested. "How about a game?"

23

"What kind?" said Erika, thoroughly ready for mischief again.

"A banister race. Whoever gets down in the least time must give the other one a cookie. Macaroons, if you have any. They're my favorites."

"I hate macaroons—they leave a bad taste in my mouth, and so do you." She squeezed her eyes into slits. "But, come on, you old macaroon. I'll play your silly game."

The raccoon shrugged. He didn't mind being called Macaroon. It sounded tasty enough to him.

For the next hour they slid swoopingly down the two-story banister, Erika carrying the raccoon on the upward journeys because he insisted on it. Neither could decide who won, so it ended in their both going into the kitchen.

The cook, a sour woman stuffed into a checked dress much too small for her, was not delighted to admit a raccoon into her kitchen. But she was afraid of Erika, and with very bad manners indeed slammed down a jar of cookies on the table.

The raccoon bowed his thanks to her, and the cook's face relaxed.

Erika grabbed two handfuls of cookies and went into the hall. Macaroon followed, his paws almost as crammed.

"I always wash before eating," he announced.

Erika made a spitting noise with her tongue and pointed to the high staircase which led to the bathroom. Macaroon reminded himself he was not here to teach her manners, quite the opposite, and humped himself up to the first floor.

He didn't need to search long because the scent of soap floated under the crack of a nearby door. He reached up the full length of his body, turned the knob, and walked in.

"Very pretty," he said to himself, admiring the rose-sprinkled wallpaper, the shining whiteness of the bathtub, and the ivory bristles of a tiny brush

dangling by the washbasin. In five minutes he was drifting tranquilly up and down the tub now filled with warm water, the cookies piled carefully beside the toothbrush.

Two hours later, after a solid nap, Macaroon emerged from what he now assumed was his room and wandered downstairs. All was quiet in the wood-paneled entrance hall. The raccoon listened for some trace of Erika so that he could go where she wasn't. It was rather a nervous business trying not to be friends with someone, like always being on guard against tigers in an open field.

Suddenly two sets of giant claws descended upon his shoulders. He yelled and leaped up so high in the air that his tail swept a lamp off a nearby table. Trembling, he took refuge under a couch and peeped cautiously out. There stood Erika, laughing so hard that the bear rug in her arms sagged to the floor.

"Fooled you that time!" she shouted. "You thought I was a savage beast, didn't you?"

Haughtily Macaroon ambled out from his hiding place and began to smooth his fur. "You're worse than a pestilence," he muttered.

"If you mean a pest, that's just what I am," responded Erika. "And now I'm having dinner served in the formal dining room. You may come too."

It wasn't long before Macaroon realized the reason

for this lapse into graciousness, because all through the meal she pelted him with small objects like green peas and bread crusts and, at the very last, walnut shells. And when the cook came to collect the plates, of course Erika let her think it was all the raccoon's fault.

The cook was not pleased. "We'll see no more of that filthy animal by tomorrow," she threatened.

"Why not, I'd like to know?" snapped Erika. "He's no affair of yours. This is my house."

"Is that right, missy? We'll just see, that's all!" and she stalked back to her kitchen.

With one hop Erika was at the long bell-pull that hung by the sideboard. She yanked it five times. Macaroon waited. Who would answer this arrogant summons?

The door swung wide and in rushed the governess. "Can't I even have any peace at mealtime?" she demanded. "You said you preferred to eat alone, and it has been a blessing to me. And now—" She caught sight of the raccoon, who eyed her firmly. "What on earth is *that* doing in your father's chair?"

"An enemy of mine," retorted Erika. "I invited him to stay with me."

"We'll see about that," said the tight-lipped Miss Minks. "After tomorrow," she added portentously.

Erika rooted herself directly in front of Miss Minks, so close that her nose almost brushed the tall woman's belt buckle. "What is all this about tomorrow? First the cook and now you. I command you to tell me!"

"No need to command anybody," said the governess with a twisted rise in her voice that made Macaroon's back hairs prickle. "Your father and mother are returning in the morning, and they'll soon put a stop to your nonsense about harboring a woods-creature in the house."

"That's not true!" said Erika, her hands clenching and unclenching behind her back. "They want me to have everything I need to keep me happy!"

"And that's perhaps why they leave you alone with cook and me for most of the year?" The sneer behind Miss Minks's words tempted Macaroon to nip holes in her stockings, but he remained motionless. This wasn't his battle or his concern, and the darker things got for Erika the better. She deserved it as payment for her utter selfishness and absolutely perfect rudeness.

"You wait!" Erika was yelling now. "You just wait! I'll have them fire you the very first thing!"

"I think not," answered the governess. "I'm the only one who has stayed with you more than three weeks in five years."

At this Erika gave such a grating roar of rage that Macaroon slid under the table for protection, and a good move it was, for suddenly the room flashed with a hail of plates and glasses that crashed haphazardly against the nearest obstacles. Then he saw Miss Minks seize Erika by the arms and drag the flurry of kicking, writhing child out of the room and up the stairs.

233467

Macaroon didn't wait for the arrival of the cook—
he was getting out, back to his forest. What if his
paws did curl in cramps as he slept in his tree-hole
all winter? What if he did get thinner and thinner
until he became a mere shadow of a raccoon? No
amount of comfort and warmth and lamb chops
was worth this stormy, hating mockery of a home.
Well, he would just help himself to that charming
brush in the bathroom and be on his way.

As he passed Erika's door he heard the shrieks dwindle to an out-of-breath kind of panting that hunted animals make when they have run too far for their strength.

This short pause was Macaroon's undoing. By the time the governess had gone down the stairs, never seeing the deep darkness of the raccoon flattened against the wall, the sound coming from behind Erika's closed door had changed. Macaroon tried very hard not to listen, but his ears were as keen as thorns and the sound crept in. Erika was crying. And even then Macaroon would not have broken his trip back to the peace and chill of his forest if his mind hadn't recognized the difference between crying for anger and crying for sadness, and Erika's was all sadness.

Irritated with himself, he gently turned the knob of Erika's door and went in.

Erika took one look at Macaroon from her red-lidded, tear-splashed eyes and spluttered, "Get out! Get out of here!"

The raccoon gazed at her solemnly, then closed the door behind him and walked to the window. He pried it up just far enough so that he could squeeze through. The sobbing and the heaving had ceased. Now came a series of sniffs and gulps and throat-clearings.

He balanced himself on the window sill, and was about to reach for the nearest branch of the tree just outside when a choky voice stopped him.

"Where are you going?" said the voice, as unlike Erika's as a lark's is unlike a gull's.

"Back home," said the raccoon, and instead of climbing into the tree, he scratched himself under the chin where it didn't itch, just to give her more time.

"I'm going with you," said the child, and without waiting for his consent, she hurriedly thrust on her heaviest sweater and tied a red scarf around her neck.

"Nobody wants me," she continued, "so I don't want anybody."

"And how do you know I want you?" asked Macaroon.

"Maybe you don't, but I'm coming with you anyway."

Something warned the raccoon that this was the instant to refuse, to tell her flatly that life in the winter forest was complicated enough without the burden of this most impossible of all impossible children. He still had a choice. He must abandon her or tame her. Then he remembered the sound that was all sadness, and he chose.

"I don't like the idea," he said, "but—well, come along." And without further delay he led the way to the stairs. "You'll be hungry before night," he whispered as they reached the front door. "You'd better go get some food from the kitchen without the cook's knowing it."

"Oh, I'll get the food all right," said Erika. "Cook

is accustomed to doing what I tell her to do."

The raccoon shook his head, doubting all over again the wisdom of his choice, but he did not use her absence to run away and leave her. In three minutes Erika, carrying a picnic basket loaded with bread, cold chicken, and cheese, appeared, and the two of them escaped unseen from the house and trotted together into the forest.

"Where is your house?" Erika said finally, after they had walked what seemed to be at least two miles.

"House?" said the raccoon. "I live in a tree."

"Oh, a tree-house."

"No. A hole in a tree."

"Is it big enough for me, too?"

"Hardly."

"Then where will I sleep?"

Macaroon wished he didn't have to answer this, because he didn't know. "We'll let that take care of itself when the time comes for sleeping," he replied, and wished he had had sense enough to adopt nobody this autumn.

"I know. I'll find a cave—the kind bears live in."

Erika's idea of how bears live had come out of a book where their houses were completely furnished with tables and chairs and hot cereal. For a while this thought kept the mounting chill of night from penetrating too far into her sweater. But when they at last arrived at the raccoon's oak tree, all she wanted was a fireplace and a cup of cocoa.

"Let's have some supper," said Macaroon, seeing the child's nose crinkle in the first stage of a sneeze. So Erika unlatched the basket, and they soon were chewing hungrily at hunks of bread with cheese between.

Erika shivered twice. "You have fur," she commented. "I haven't."

"I'd lend you some of mine, but I can't," said the raccoon, quite worried now and determined to urge her to return to her house. He had just opened his mouth to speak, when out of the deepening shadows of tree-trunk and underbrush limped the lame fox.

"Thought I smelled supper," said the fox, and he made a grab with his teeth at something in the basket.

Erika lunged at him and smashed the lid shut,

40

scraping the fox's nose hurtfully. "You can't have any!" she shouted, her own face more vixenish than the fox's.

The fox sat down on his haunches at a distance of five yards and looked sorrowfully at the raccoon, the girl, and the concealed chicken. "I'm very empty," he said. Then he looked directly at Erika. "You belong to people, don't you?"

"Am I a person, you mean? Yes, of course. Why?"

"I thought so. Just like all the others. You don't know how to share a chicken. Or anything else," he added, licking his lame foot.

Macaroon gave Erika a steely signal with both eyes. Erika was puzzled. She watched Macaroon carefully divide his bread and cheese into two portions and hand one to the fox. Imperiously she waved back Macaroon's bread and cheese and dipped her hand into the basket and offered the fox a fat brown chicken leg.

But this time the fox did not grab. He hesitated. "No tricks?" he said, his nose quivering.

"No tricks," said Erika, and stretched out her hand and the chicken.

"Thank you," said the fox, and he quietly accepted the leg and began to crunch the sweet and buttery meat.

By the time the basket was vacant it was true dark. Only Erika's white skin and the fox's tawny coat gleamed a little lighter than the blackened background of the woods.

"I sometimes smell snow nowadays," said the fox, to make conversation.

"Not tonight, surely," said the raccoon, sitting as close to Erika as he could because he knew the cold was entering her bones.

"No. But soon. Guess I'll be going along now."
But before he could say a final good-night, the raccoon had an idea.

"Could you let Erika sleep in your den with you?
It would be warmer than just nowhere."

"Certainly," said the fox, content to return the
favor of the chicken. "Follow me."

"I'm not going without Macaroon," said Erika,
firmly.

Macaroon stifled a giant sigh and trotted behind
the procession of two. After all, he didn't really
mind, for he loved to adventure through the night.

The fox's earth was just a few yards distant, and
he plunged down and into the hole almost before
Erika could spot it. She wriggled herself through a
short tunnel and then popped out into a more spa-
cious underground dugout.

"It smells!" she exclaimed, covering her nose with
one hand.

"Naturally," said Macaroon, wishing for the hun-
dredth time he had not accepted the job of reforming
this impossible child. "Of musk and delicious fox-
scent." He poked her in the ribs with one elbow and

was just about to pinch her ankle when she got the point.

"It's lovely," she added hastily and breathed as shallowly as she could.

"Thank you," said the fox, and he curled himself into a round and closed his eyes.

Erika was silent for a few moments. Then she stretched full-length on the warm earth and whispered in Macaroon's nearest ear, "Do you think they've missed me at my house yet?"

"I'd guess they have," answered Macaroon. "Want to go back now?"

"Never!" hissed Erika. "The cook hates me, Miss Minks hates me, and so do the other two."

Macaroon knew she meant her father and mother. "I doubt that," he said as sturdily as a whisper would allow.

"I don't. If they didn't, why don't they ever come back except when they feel like it or are out of jobs? It's never because of me. Why, they didn't even turn up for Christmas. Is that what you call loving?"

Macaroon had very positive ideas on this subject, but he didn't want to share them with this child who was really no better off than an orphan. "They are coming tomorrow."

"For reasons of their own. Oh, maybe they'll be worried for a few days, but later, a week or so from now, they will look at each other and one of them might say, 'Remember when we used to have a child called Erika?' and the other will answer and say, 'Yes. Yes, I do. Wonder what ever befell her?' "

"Well, I'll tell you what is befalling me," said Macaroon. "Sleep." He waved his tail in good-night and turned his head in the direction of the entrance to the den where the air should have been fresher and wasn't, and soon joined the fox in equal dreaming.

Erika had no other choice than to shut her eyes, but before she capsized into unconsciousness she thought that just maybe she heard faraway shouts.

It was not yet dawn when the raccoon was jolted awake by the sharp strike of the fox's paw. "They're coming! They're coming!" half-barked the fox.

Macaroon, quickened completely out of sleep, spoke back. "Who? Who's coming?"

"The dogs! They're coming to get me!"

"Be quiet!" ordered Macaroon, and he listened with such concentration that to his ears, too, arrived the distant, excited yelps of hounds. "But this isn't hunting country!" he exclaimed.

"Used to be in my grandfather's time," said the fox. "He told me. What can I do? I am lame. What on earth can I do?"

Macaroon flicked his tail across Erika's face and she came alert almost as quickly as an animal. "What is it?" she said, aware that trouble had entered the den.

"The dogs are coming to get me!" said the fox, his breath already shortened.

"Nonsense," said the girl. "It's me they're after. Nobody hunts around here. In the first place nobody owns any riding horses." Then her face took on the same squeezed look as the fox's. "But they're not going to catch me." She looked at the fox and the raccoon and something in her eyes flowered for the first time; she was asking a favor of someone else and she didn't know how.

Macaroon glanced at the fox, and the same answer was in his triangular face. "We will help you," he said. "Especially me. You shared your food with us. The fox shared his home. Now it's my turn." He raised his arms over his head as though addressing a parliament. "Now listen. The dogs have undoubtedly been given your scent, Erika, and in a few minutes they will arrive at the fox's earth." He pointed to the fox. "Just before they get here you will go above ground and show yourself. No dog could ever resist chasing a fox. Then you will lead them off and away from here while Erika and I find another hiding place. We'll have to break her scent, so that

49

means getting to the brook in the woods and wading downstream. You must give us time enough for that."

"I'll try," said the fox gallantly. "But how do I shake off the dogs?"

"When the people behind the dogs discover they are chasing a fox, they'll call them off."

"I most fervently hope so," said the fox.

"Stop hoping and start running," instructed the raccoon. "Those hounds are almost upon us."

With a salute of his bushy tail the fox vanished from the den. Macaroon and Erika could hear a tangled confusion of yips and barks and scrambling as the dogs changed course. When the upper regions were nearly silent, Macaroon nudged Erika. "We must go now," and they pushed themselves through the burrow and regained the outer world. A thick mist obscured all but the nearest trees. "We're in luck," whispered the raccoon. "Pick me up and I'll tell you where to go. It will be faster that way."

Erika grabbed the raccoon in her arms and began to race toward the center of the forest. Roots and ruts conspired to make her stumble, but she did not

decrease her pace. "Keep going!" encouraged the raccoon, uncomfortably mashed against her collarbone but resisting any complaint. "The stream is only a few yards more."

And when Erika finally reached the banks of the narrow waterway she almost fell in. "Put me down," said Macaroon. "Now follow me." He half-paddled, half-walked through the rough rush of water, Erika splashing behind him.

Once the chorus of dogs whirled just a hundred feet away, but the fox still had them in hand.

"How much longer?" wheezed the child. "I'm freezing and I've cut my shins all over."

"See that oak ahead?" spoke back the raccoon, still forging onward. "That's our refuge."

Erika couldn't see the oak because the fog was as dense as smoke, but she trusted the raccoon to know. At last she saw him clamber up the steep bank and disappear behind a thicket.

She stepped upward, slipped on the damp mud, and slid back into the stream. Drenched and shuddery, she drew herself upright again and, seizing the long grasses that beckoned at the top of the shallow

ridge, hoisted and yanked and heaved until she found herself flat on her stomach on the wet ground. She sat up. "Macaroon, where are you?" she called, afraid to speak too loud in case the dogs were near.

Then she saw him, tall against the tree, and flopped down beside him.

Macaroon didn't wait for her to catch her breath. "I'm very worried," he said gravely.

"About me?"

"No, not about you. About the fox. He's got a game leg and is no longer young."

"What could happen to him? You said that as soon as they find out the dogs are chasing a fox they will call them off."

"That's what I said, but I'm not at all sure it's happening that way." Macaroon's ears drooped and his paws churned nervously together in the movements of washing. Then his paws stilled and he looked at Erika with such intensity and for so long that her cheeks began to redden. She knew the raccoon was waiting for her to say something and also that that something must be just the right thing, not a comment on the weather or even a discussion of the problem. She tried to break away from his deep, deep look, but she couldn't. She tried not to think, but thoughts like the first approach of sky-borne birds winged into her mind, flying so close she could almost hear the wind's flap on their feathers. Why had she run away? Because no one loved her and she was forced to be cross all the time. Why was she so cross? Why had she made life a torture for both the cook and Miss Minks? Why was she the way she was? How was she? The word loomed like a hawk and pounced: impossible.

Erika didn't know why, but suddenly she felt like crying, not for sadness but for another kind of feeling that made her body strong and new. "Come on!" she cried. "We have to find the fox!"

Just at that instant such a tempest of legs and tails and snarls and barks whirled around them that Erika was knocked flat on her back. The five dogs scrabbled over and around her, intent on bringing down a very ragged, tawny specter of a fox. She raised herself half up, shoved into the center of the furious tangle, and encircled the exhausted fox within her arms.

But what was the high, shrilling war cry that rang in her ears? Even the triumphant hounds checked their violence. It was Macaroon, standing straight up on his hind legs, daring the five great beasts to do battle. The first one who advanced never even saw what tore a hunk of fur from his chest. The next received a gash the length of his foreleg.

Erika, still holding the fox, scrambled to one side and set him on all four feet. "Can you make it to your den?" she asked.

The fox's foam-splattered mouth formed one word, "Yes," and he staggered off into the mist.

Still the beleaguered raccoon held off the dogs, thrusting swift as the blade of a sword at his nearest attackers. But Erika knew that surrounded as tightly as he was, it wouldn't be long before he fell under their jaws.

She ignored the cuts and bruises that splotched her hands and legs, and picking up a gnarled stick, she whacked at the dogs as hard as she could. But they were too intent on the slaughter of one of their oldest enemies, and the circle around the raccoon shrank like the closing of a noose.

"Nobody's going to hurt Macaroon!" she shouted, not caring for anything or anybody except the courageous little animal whose left ear was now scarlet with blood. "Nobody! Nobody!" She kicked her way through the dogs, seized him around the stomach, and held him high over her head. "Now kill *me* if you want to, but you'll never get Macaroon!"

Their prey removed from reaching distance, the dogs crouched and growled and paced, but did not touch the girl. Erika, so shaky inside that her backbone seemed to be turning to clots of sand, walked right through the pack and started out of the forest. Twice she felt the knick of teeth at her heels and once she heard her dress rip at the edges, but she continued to walk, slowly and steadily through the trees, Macaroon like a furry umbrella above her.

"Don't be afraid," she said to him as they passed through the last barrier of tree-trunks and into the meadow that led to her house. "We are going home."

Macaroon carefully said nothing, and it wasn't entirely because she gripped him so tightly around the middle he could scarcely breathe. He was so proud of his adopted child there were no words at all to say, not ever.

They had no sooner gained the gates of the mansion than the dogs fell away and a small crowd of people poured toward them from around the corner of the house. One was Erika's mother. Another was her father. Even Miss Minks was there, sniffling into a very wet handkerchief. The others stood back with very trembly grins on their faces.

And just before they met, Erika halted and put Macaroon on the ground. "Are you all right?" she asked so no one else could hear. The little animal nodded and put his left paw into her right hand. Together they faced this new problem of people.

Two people, a man and a woman, walked forward until they were within three feet of the child and the raccoon. They hesitated, looked uncertainly at one another, and then the woman put out her hand toward Erika as though she weren't sure she should touch her. Macaroon felt Erika's hand tighten around his paw. He raised his nose and brushed the back of her hand twice, trying to tell her to forgive. She understood, and extended her free arm to the woman.

Suddenly the child was enveloped in such a hugging and laughing and crying that Macaroon slid his paw from between her fingers. Now they were all three talking so fast, their words so jumbled and mixed and happy, that Macaroon had to laugh too.

Then he knew it was time for him to leave. Erika had a family now, a family she was ready to love and live with. She wouldn't need him. He smiled a little wryly. Well, maybe his fur would thicken during the sleep-drugged nights of snow and frost. He shrugged, and then he knew his winter would be a good one. Just the thought of Erika, herself at last, would keep him warm and comforted.

He quietly turned about-face and said a silent
farewell to his friend. He would miss her, more than
all the rest lumped together, and he knew at that
very instant that he would never again adopt anyone else. Erika was the last and the best.

But before his first step was taken, before he even
swallowed the first gulp of loneliness, someone
kissed him right on top of his head and whispered
in his torn ear, "Macaroon, we're both home. And
do you know what we'll do together first thing tomorrow morning? Fill a basket with the most wonder-
ful feast in the world and invite the fox to share it."

Macaroon did not speak. Instead, he smiled
straight into the wide happiness of her suddenly
lovely eyes.